SPORTS GREAT
BARRY
BONDS

—*Sports Great Books* —

Sports Great Jim Abbott
(ISBN 0-89490-395-0)

Sports Great Troy Aikman
(ISBN 0-89490-593-7)

Sports Great Charles Barkley
(ISBN 0-89490-386-1)

Sports Great Larry Bird
(ISBN 0-89490-368-3)

Sports Great Barry Bonds
(ISBN 0-89490-595-3)

Sports Great Bobby Bonilla
(ISBN 0-89490-417-5)

Sports Great Roger Clemens
(ISBN 0-89490-284-9)

Sports Great John Elway
(ISBN 0-89490-282-2)

Sports Great Patrick Ewing
(ISBN 0-89490-369-1)

Sports Great Steffi Graf
(ISBN 0-89490-597-X)

Sports Great Orel Hershiser
(ISBN 0-89490-389-6)

Sports Great Bo Jackson
(ISBN 0-89490-281-4)

**Sports Great Magic Johnson
(Revised and Expanded)**
(ISBN 0-89490-348-9)

Sports Great Michael Jordan
(ISBN 0-89490-370-5)

Sports Great Mario Lemieux
(ISBN 0-89490-596-1)

Sports Great Karl Malone
(ISBN 0-89490-599-6)

Sports Great Joe Montana
(ISBN 0-89490-371-3)

Sports Great Hakeem Olajuwon
(ISBN 0-89490-372-1)

Sports Great Shaquille O'Neal
(ISBN 0-89490-594-5)

Sports Great Kirby Puckett
(ISBN 0-89490-392-6)

Sports Great Jerry Rice
(ISBN 0-89490-419-1)

Sports Great Cal Ripken, Jr.
(ISBN 0-89490-387-X)

Sports Great David Robinson
(ISBN 0-89490-373-X)

Sports Great Nolan Ryan
(ISBN 0-89490-394-2)

Sports Great Barry Sanders
(ISBN 0-89490-418-3)

Sports Great John Stockton
(ISBN 0-89490-598-8)

Sports Great Darryl Strawberry
(ISBN 0-89490-291-1)

Sports Great Isiah Thomas
(ISBN 0-89490-374-8)

Sports Great Herschel Walker
(ISBN 0-89490-207-5)

SPORTS GREAT BARRY BONDS

Michael J. Sullivan

—Sports Great Books—

ENSLOW PUBLISHERS, INC.
44 Fadem Road   P.O. Box 38
Box 699   Aldershot
Springfield, N.J. 07081 Hants GU12 6BP
U.S.A.   U.K.

Library of Congress Cataloging-in-Publication Data

Sullivan, Michael John, 1960–
    Sports great Barry Bonds / Michael J. Sullivan
        p. cm. — (Sports great books)
    Includes index.
    ISBN 0-89490-595-3
    1. Bonds, Barry, 1964– —Juvenile literature. 2. Baseball players—United
States—Biography—Juvenile literature. [1. Bonds, Barry, 1964– . 2. Baseball players. 3.
Afro-Americans—Biography.] I. Title. II. Series.
GV865.B637S85 1995
796.357'092—dc20
[B]
                                            94-37930
                                               CIP
                                             AC

Printed in the United States of America

10 9 8 7 6 5 4 3 2 1

Illustration Credits: AP/Wide World Photos, p. 16; *San Francisco Chronicle*, pp.
28, 30, 32, 37, 42, 46, 48, 58; Martha Jane Stanton, pp. 8, 10, 18, 20, 22, 26, 38,
40, 50, 54, 56.

Cover Illustration: *San Francisco Chronicle.*

Contents

Chapter 1

The crowd of 51,860 at Dodger Stadium was joyous on October 1, 1993, even though their beloved Los Angeles Dodgers were not in the pennant race. They had the next best thing—a chance to help stop the rival San Francisco Giants from winning the Western Division crown of the National League. Manager Tommy Lasorda's team had one goal—not to let the Giants win the division!

The Giants, leaders of the division for most of the season, were tied with the Atlanta Braves. Now there were only three games left in the season. The two teams had won an amazing total of 101 games. The Braves were playing an easier opponent, the Colorado Rockies. The Rockies were in their first major-league year. Most baseball experts believed that the Braves would not lose one game to the Rockies, since Atlanta hadn't lost one to Colorado all season! The Braves were also playing at home, while the Giants were playing in front of a hostile Dodger crowd.

The Dodgers were playing well in the first game of the three-game series. They quickly jumped all over San

Barry Bonds is the star hitter for the San Francisco Giants.

Francisco pitcher John Burkett for three runs in the first. Brett Butler, Jose Offerman, and Dave Hansen each scored a run for Los Angeles. It was not going to get any easier for the Giants. Los Angeles felt confident that they could beat their California rivals. The Dodgers added another run in the fourth to take a 4–0 advantage off Burkett, who had won twenty-one games so far that season.

The Dodger crowd roared as each Los Angeles runner crossed home plate. The Giants were becoming nervous; Ramon Martinez was on the mound for Los Angeles. Martinez was a young pitcher who threw either very well or very poorly. Tonight he was pitching well.

Barry Bonds, the National League's most feared hitter, was going to change that in the third. One of his teammates, Darren Lewis, drove a ball that skidded past Hansen at third base down the left field line. Usually, a ball hit down the left field line is a double, but Lewis's speed enabled him to make it to third base. The Giants were desperate. Time was running out. They had to take every extra base they could.

One out later, Will Clark, the Giants' first baseman, came to the plate with Lewis still at third base. Martinez tried to slip a fastball past Clark on the outside of the plate. Clark was not fooled. The left-handed hitter slapped the ball down the left field line. Lewis scored, and Clark made it to second base. San Francisco now trailed, 4–1.

The Dodger crowd was uneasy. They started getting worried when Giants third baseman Matt Williams lined a base hit to left field. It was hit so hard that Clark could only make it to third base. Usually, on a base hit to the outfield, the runner is able to score from second base.

Then the Giants' best hitter, Barry Bonds, moved up to the plate. The Dodger fans were on the edge of their seats. They were nervous and anxious. They had good reason to worry.

Barry watches as another of his home runs leaves the stadium.

Barry Bonds had hit 44 homers already that season and had driven in 116 runs.

Martinez looked for a sign from catcher Kirt Manwaring. Barry's bat went *crack* as it whacked Martinez's fastball toward right center. It was high. The crowd in the bleachers stood as Dodgers center fielder Butler raced toward the wall. If Butler caught the ball, then both Clark and Williams could advance a base at their own risk. As Butler was running, Clark moved back to third to tag. Williams moved back to first to do the same thing.

Barry's forty-fifth homer of the year landed in the bleachers among the stunned Dodgers fans. The game was tied 4–4. There was silence in Dodger Stadium now. The Giants were alive again!

At the end of the inning, pitcher John Burkett raced out to the mound with his arms flapping high. The Giants were confident again. Barry Bonds had only just begun to hit.

"There's no ball that he can't hit out if he gets the big part of the bat on it," Giants coach Bobby Bonds said. "He can hit it no matter where it is."

The game was still tied at the top of the fifth inning; San Francisco's best hitters were coming up. Clark, who already had two hits, hit Martinez's pitch into right field for a single. Williams was the next batter. He could sense that Martinez was tiring. Martinez's fastball was not as fast as it had been in the first two innings. Williams hit Martinez's fastball down the left field line. Clark raced to third base, while Williams made it to second for a double. The Dodger crowd was worried. Barry Bonds was up again.

Los Angeles manager Tommy Lasorda was also worried. He came out of the dugout and called in a left-handed pitcher named Omar Daal. Lasorda told Daal to be careful with the left-handed–hitting Barry Bonds. Since there was nobody for the Giants on first base, many people at the game, including Barry's father, thought Daal would intentionally walk Bonds.

"At that point," Bobby Bonds said, "I don't know if I [would] pitch to Barry. Let's put it that way. And I know Barry better than anybody."

Bobby was right. After all, he's Barry's father. Barry wouldn't disappoint his dad. Daal threw two curveballs that landed way outside and in the dirt. Barry was patient; he wasn't going to swing at any bad pitch. Lasorda now thought that maybe he should tell Daal to give the intentional walk; but he changed his mind. "Listen, I'm not going to walk anybody right there," Lasorda said later. "You're asking this guy to throw strikes (the next hitter was Willie McGee, a very good hitter) with nobody out and the bases loaded. That's not good baseball."

Or was it? After all, Barry Bonds was considered the best player and hitter in the National League; and he proved it on the next pitch. *Craaack!* The ball soared high toward the bleachers again. Butler again ran after the ball. Both Williams and Clark watched in case the ball was caught. It wasn't! Barry Bonds had hit his forty-sixth homer of the season, and now he had 123 RBI.

Barry knew the tough Dodgers weren't going to quit. Even though the Giants had a 7–4 lead, San Francisco always needed more runs against the Dodgers. The Giants still led in the seventh inning. Clark again was able to get on base with a hit. He advanced to second after Williams grounded out. Barry Bonds came up again. Steve Wilson was now pitching for Los Angeles. Barry hit a line drive into center field. Clark scored, and the Giants led, 8–4. It was a run San Francisco was going to need.

The Dodgers had scored one run in the seventh inning. Giants reliever Rod Beck, their best pitcher coming out of the bull pen, was having trouble with the Dodgers in the ninth inning. The Dodgers then scared the Giants in the ninth inning by adding two more runs. The score was now 8–7. Giants manager Dusty Baker had confidence in Beck, so he didn't take him out.

The confidence paid off. Beck was able to get the last Dodger out and the Giants won their 102nd game of the year. The Braves won too, against the Rockies. San Francisco was alive one more day because of Barry Bonds, who hit 2 homers and had a career-high 7 RBI. "It's amazing," said Burkett, who won his twenty-second game with just seven defeats. "It's an amazing story. I hope we can hold on to it for two more days."

Thanks to Barry Bonds and his magical bat, the Giants had that opportunity.

Chapter 2

Barry Lamar Bonds was born on July 24, 1964, in Riverside, California. As he grew up, he was taught the finer points of playing baseball. His father, Bobby Bonds, had spent fourteen seasons in the major leagues. Bobby played with several teams, including the Giants (while Willie Mays was there) and the New York Yankees. Just like his son, Barry, Bobby had terrific power and speed. Bobby hit 332 homers in his career, a feat that Barry may duplicate someday. Like Barry, Bobby was also a great defensive outfielder. They are the only father and son ever to win the Rawlings Gold Glove Award, which is given to the best defensive players.

Bobby was one of the better ballplayers back in the 1970s. The big question was: Could little Barry be as good, or better? "Barry was hitting at the age of one year," Bobby said, "but he perfected his baseball swing at the age of two. At one, he was a .260 hitter; at two he was a .320 hitter. He could knock the starch out of the ball. I'll tell you that."

Growing up in California, Barry had the best training a youngster could get. First, he had a great coach for a father.

Barry's godfather, Willie Mays, is a baseball legend. Mays' 660 homers places him third on the all-time list behind Hank Aaron and Babe Ruth.

Second, his godfather was Hall of Famer Willie Mays, who spent a lot of time working with Barry on his game. It was the dream of every young boy who wanted to be a major-league baseball player, but Barry was living it!

"Barry needed to work like everybody else," Bobby said. "But it was at the age of one where I felt he had the making of a ballplayer."

Despite having wonderful baseball teachers, Barry still had to spend time in school. This meant being away from his father quite a lot when Bobby was off on road trips. It was not easy for Barry. When Bobby could get to Barry's high school games, he would sit in his car at the field so his presence would not disrupt the game. Barry also became very close to his grandfather, Robert Bonds. "He was just, like, my best friend," Barry said of his grandfather, who was a construction worker in Riverside. "He was just an old man who was born in the times when black people couldn't do a lot. He used to have to walk on the other side of the street. But he never had any jealousy. Never any prejudice. No remorse. No nothing. Just the nicest man I've ever met in my whole life."

Barry loved his grandfather very much. "My grandfather would watch my baseball games," Barry said. "All the time. No matter what I was doing, no matter where I was, he'd go to my baseball games because my dad was never there. So I'd visit my grandfather all the time."

When Barry was about eleven or twelve years old, people began talking about him. They said that he was a terrific young ballplayer, better than most high school players. Barry knew that someday he was going to be a major-league ballplayer. Barry played high school ball at Serra High School in San Mateo, California. He played center field in his senior year and hit an incredible .467 in 1982.

Barry helps a young player with batting practice. Growing up, Barry had the best teachers: his father, Bobby, and his godfather, Willie Mays.

"The guy was bad," said Ray McDonald, who played third base on the 1982 team with Barry. "I still can't hit one out of Central Park in San Mateo and he was doing it in high school. His outfield play [today], though, has really surprised me. You can tell he's really worked at it."

Barry Bonds's high school team was made up of some very good players, but none were as good as Barry. "That team in 1982 had a lot of good players," said Dave Canziani, who played first base that year. "A lot of people were drafted. Barry could have done anything he wanted; he's a great athlete."

Barry was drafted by the San Francisco Giants. He decided, though, to put major-league baseball on hold and to attend Arizona State University. He wanted to get an education at one of the better universities in the country while also polishing his baseball skills. It worked out well for Barry. He studied criminal justice, learning about why people commit crimes.

Barry played baseball for the Arizona State Sun Devils, and he was named to the All-Pac Ten team as a freshman. He was also honored with the Most Valuable Player award of the NCAA West II Regional Tournament. Thanks to Barry Bonds and his hot bat, Arizona State advanced to the 1983 College World Series.

"I want people to notice me on the baseball field," Barry said. "I want them to say, 'Barry Bonds is the best player there is.' But that just doesn't happen. An athlete has to make it happen."

During this time a tragic event occurred in Barry's life. "When I first got to college, I had an off day so I drove from Arizona State to see my grandfather," Barry said. "Then I got back that morning and my mom called me and told me my grandfather died. I said, 'No, he didn't—I just saw him a

Barry waits for a line drive. From the time he was a young boy, he worked to develop the concentration and skill of a major league player.

couple of hours ago.' She said he died in his chair watching baseball games of me."

Barry's grandmother gave him a cross on a chain that was his grandfather's. To this day, Barry keeps that cross with him in memory of Robert Bonds, one of his closest friends.

"My grandfather's part of me," Barry said. "He's the one who keeps me going at times, you know? Most of the time. That's my inspiration. To grow up in those times and not have any hatred, nothing—it's incredible. The pain he's probably been through his whole life."

Barry tried to forget his own pain. His hard work and determination kept him on track. After his freshman year, people noticed Barry Bonds, but it was his second year that made people believe that he was probably the best player in college baseball. He was named again to the All-Pac Ten team, and he helped Arizona State return to the College World Series. In this round-robin event, Barry tied an NCAA tournament record by posting seven consecutive base hits. Even during college, Barry reflected on his father's advice when he was growing up: "Intensity slows you down," Barry said. "When you get too wound up, when you get too excited, your muscles have a tendency to slow down. It's a lot easier when you're relaxed. Like my dad always says to me, 'If you're relaxed, and there's a fly buzzing around your ear, you can go like that and grab it fast.' You don't even think about it. And that's what I try to do with myself. I just try to relax enough to visualize as many positive things as possible."

Positive things were happening for Barry Bonds at Arizona State. Bonds played well again in his junior season, and he was named for the third time to the All-Pac Ten team. He hit .368 in 62 games. He also homered 23 times and had 66 RBI. He led the Sun Devils in both categories. However, for the first time since Barry came to Arizona State, his team

21

As early as his freshman year in college, Barry became known as a powerful home run hitter.

didn't go to the world series. It gave him a bad feeling. "When the media categorize you as one of the best, you never really get that elite class unless you win," he says. "There were guys who weren't in Ernie Banks's class who you hear about because they won."

Barry put up magical numbers during his three seasons at Arizona State. He hit .347, homered 45 times, had 175 RBI, and showed his speed by stealing 57 bases. He was named to the Sporting News College Baseball All-American team.

Barry Bonds didn't have any time to enjoy his wonderful statistics. In his junior year he had to decide whether to return for his senior season or to sign with a major-league team. There was no doubt that Barry was going to be drafted. He was selected by the Pittsburgh Pirates in the first round of the June 1985 free agent draft. He was the sixth player taken. He did sign this time with Pittsburgh, and he was assigned to the Pirates' Prince William club, in the Class A Carolina League. Barry Bonds was only a few short steps away from realizing his dream of being a major-league player.

Chapter 3

Barry Bonds was confident. He knew he was as good as any other player in the minor leagues, and he was going to prove it. He played in 71 games for Prince William in 1985 and hit .299. He hit 13 homers and drove in 37 runs. Barry also proved he was a serious threat on the bases. He stole 15 bases. "If you know me, you know I always find something that I feel I have to prove," Barry said. "Some people accuse me of having a chip on my shoulder, but that's part of what makes me tick. I like to have something that drives me."

It's been that way for Barry since he was a youngster. He grew up hearing about how terrific his father, Bobby, and his godfather, Willie Mays, were when they played the game. From the day Barry Bonds picked up his bat when he was a member of Prince William, he was focused on getting to the major leagues. He wanted to show his father and godfather just how good he was.

During his first year in the minors, Barry showed that it wouldn't be long before he would have that opportunity. He startled minor-league fans in North Carolina by belting 3

Barry races to steal second base.

homers in a game against Durham on July 19, 1985. Barry seemed to like hitting against Durham; he hit 3 more homers in three consecutive at bats over July 26 and July 27. For his extraordinary performances, Bonds was named Player of the Month for July in the Carolina League.

Barry played the following season at the Pirates' Triple-A farm club in Hawaii. While in Hawaii, Barry batted .311. He hit 7 homers and drove in 37 runs. He also continued to impress onlookers with his base-stealing ability. He swiped 16 bases that year.

"Barry just wanted his due," said Pittsburgh manager Jim Leyland. "That's all. What drives him to greatness is that he wants to prove to the world every day that he is the best."

He was only there for forty-four games; then Pittsburgh called him up to the big leagues. Barry convinced the Pirates' management that he was ready for that chance in the major leagues. He made it to the majors on May 30, 1986. His first base hit came off the Dodgers' left-handed Rick Honeycutt on May 31. Four days later, Barry faced Braves veteran right-hander Craig McMurtry in Atlanta. McMurtry was a crafty pitcher who threw at different speeds to keep the batters off balance, so they would never know what kind of pitch to expect.

Barry had read about McMurtry. Every ball club sends the hitters scouting reports about every major-league pitcher, so Barry was prepared. McMurtry tried to work him away with curveballs. Barry missed on his first two tries. With the count in his favor, Barry was looking for a certain pitch. He knew that McMurtry was too smart a pitcher to try and throw him a fastball inside, so he looked for one outside. *Craaack!* Barry shocked McMurtry by going the other way. The ball landed beyond the fence in left field, and Barry Bonds had his first major-league homer.

In his rookie season with the Pittsburgh Pirates, Barry established himself as an all-around player.

Barry impressed many major-league pitchers in his rookie year. He played only 113 games, but he led all National League rookies in homers (16), RBI (48), stolen bases (36), and walks (65). His 36 steals were the second highest number ever by a Pirate rookie; Omar Moreno had 53 in 1977. Barry's 16 homers were the most hit by a Pittsburgh first-year man since Al Oliver smacked 17 in 1969. More importantly, with Barry leading off the Pirates' batting, manager Jim Leyland had speed and power at the top of his order. Barry led off a game three times by hitting homers.

"I try to make sure I don't get booed," Barry said. "An athlete has to make it happen. The players know who's a con artist and who isn't. They realize that you don't have to like me, but I'm going to try to make you respect me."

Respect for Barry Bonds continued to grow in 1987. For four straight games between August 18 and August 21, he hit a home run in each contest. He became only the second Pirate in their rich history to hit at least 20 homers and steal 20 bases in a season. (Dave Parker did it in 1978 and 1979.)

Barry showed his speed and power in one at bat that year against the Phillies' left-handed Shane Rawley, smashing a long drive toward the center field wall that just missed being a home run. It bounced off the wall and away from the Philadelphia outfielders. Barry raced around first, then second, then third, and slid safely into home before the throw from the outfield got to the catcher.

Barry Bonds was certainly helping the Pirates. They weren't the best team in the National League, but they were closing in on the Mets as a threat in the Eastern Division. In 1987, Barry finished with 25 homers, 59 RBI, and 32 stolen bases. He was quickly being recognized as one of the more dangerous leadoff hitters in the National League.

Barry Bonds is a dedicated player. At times, he has played despite injury.

Barry Bonds proved he was dangerous in 1988. He led off a game with a homer eight times while hitting .347 (42 for 121) in the first inning. "Could a fan ask for anything more," asked Jim Leyland. "No one gives the fans more for their money than Barry. He is beyond dollar value."

Barry was named the Player of the Week in the National League between April 11 and April 17, when he had 4 homers. Three times he belted 2 homers in a game. He had Pittsburgh's longest hitting streak of the season, with 11. However, on June 17, while playing against the St. Louis Cardinals, Barry hurt his left knee. He decided that the team needed him, so he played, even though he was in pain.

Barry Bonds finished 1988 by hitting .283. He hit 24 homers and drove in 58 runs—good numbers for a leadoff batter. Barry stole 17 bases, but his left knee was hurting him most of the year. He had surgery on his knee on September 28.

Barry worked hard during the off-season to get himself in shape for 1989. Fans were expecting more of him and the Pirates. Pittsburgh had yet to win a division title with him in the lineup.

Barry wanted to win more than anybody else; he played in almost every game in 1989 (159 out of 162). Again the Pirates didn't win the division. Pitchers around the National League were starting to realize that Barry was a dangerous hitter; he was walked intentionally twenty-two times. This was the fourth-highest number in the National League, and the most for a leadoff batter. Barry only hit .248. He seemed to be trying too hard to help the Pirates, hitting 19 homers and driving in 58 runs. He also stole 32 bases, but people were pitching around him in 1989. Something had to be done.

Barry Bonds appeared in the leadoff slot fourteen times in 1990. Leyland moved him permanently to the number five position in the batting order in late May. Pitchers could not

Barry robs fans of a souvenir ball.

pitch around Barry in that position. The Pirates usually had a good batter behind him to discourage pitchers from walking him.

Barry became the first Pirate ever to hit 30 or more homers and steal 30 or more bases in a season. He led the National League with his slugging percentage of .565 and his 93 walks. Despite the walks, batting number five in the order meant that more runners were on base for him. He didn't disappoint Leyland and the Pirates. He drove in 114 runners and hit 33 homers. Barry also scored 104 runs and stole 52 bases. Leyland's gamble had worked!

Barry also proved that his glove was just as shiny as his bat. He had a fielding percentage of .983 and had 14 assists. He tied the Mets' Kevin McReynolds for most assists in the National League. What made him even more happy was that the Pirates won the Eastern Division title. Barry Bonds would finally compete in the playoffs in the major leagues. Unfortunately for Pittsburgh and Barry, the Pirates were eliminated by the Cincinnati Reds. Barry did not have a good series. He had only 3 hits in 18 at bats.

However, nobody forgot about what a great season Barry Bonds had. He was named the National League Most Valuable Player and Sporting News Major League Player of the Year. In addition, he was honored with his first Gold Glove, which is given to the best player at each position for fielding excellence. He had only one thought after the season—to work harder in the off-season in preparation for 1991. He wanted to play even better than he had in 1990.

Chapter 4

Barry Bonds was disappointed by his 1991 performance. He was determined to work even harder, and he did, but sometimes even hard work will not get a player through a slump. In his first 100 at bats of the 1991 season, he had only 17 hits and a .170 batting average. Barry was frustrated, but he was even more determined than ever to overcome his slump.

In his next 126 games, Barry hit .322 with 23 homers and 102 RBI. His statistics in some categories outpaced his 1990 MVP figures. In July, he hit .362 with 6 homers, 29 RBI, 20 runs scored, and 15 stolen bases in 27 games. He was named the National League Player of the Month. When Barry's bat became hotter in the summer, the Pirates regained their winning form and captured the Eastern Division for the second year in a row. Then, in the playoffs, the Pirates lost an exciting seven-game series to the Atlanta Braves. Barry struggled again at the plate. He had only 4 hits in 27 at bats.

Barry was second in the voting for the National League MVP. However, he was again named by the *Sporting News* as the league's best player. Barry also won his second straight

Gold Glove for his 13 assists and excellent outfield play. He became the first Pirate since Willie Stargell (1972–73) to have back-to-back 100 RBI seasons. Barry Bonds was now known as the best player in the National League. "Barry Bonds belongs in a higher league," former New York Mets manager Jeff Torborg said.

Barry Bonds never enjoyed listening to compliments. He worked hard in the off-season and wanted to avoid a slow start like the one he had the year before. Whatever he did in the winter months, it worked! In April 1992, Barry hit .317 with 7 homers and 17 RBI in 18 games. Halfway through the baseball season, he was named a starter in the All-Star game for the first time. He had a double and scored a run in that game, which was held at Jack Murphy Stadium in San Diego.

Barry finished the season by hitting .311. He belted 34 homers and had 103 RBI. Barry also showed his speed with 39 stolen bases. He was again named the National League's MVP for the second time in three years.

Because of Barry's effort in the regular season, the Pirates won the Eastern Division for the third year in a row. The Pirates again met the Atlanta Braves, just as they had the year before. The Pirates headed home after seven games, while the Braves played in the World Series. However, Barry had his best postseason performance, hitting .261. He had one homer and 2 RBI, had 6 hits, and was walked 6 times.

Barry's league championship appearance would be the last time he played a game as a Pirate. Despite his success with the Pirates, Barry Bonds felt he needed a change. He was a free agent after the season and had several big offers. His heart was still in the San Francisco Bay area where he had grown up and played high school ball, so he accepted the Giants' six-year, $43 million contract. The transition was easy for him. "It happened so well," he said. "The way the fans took

Barry jokes with teammate Erik Johnson. Barry's fellow players accepted him right away when he joined the San Francisco Giants.

For every one of Barry's home runs, RBI, and stolen bases, he donates money to charity.

me in and especially the way my teammates accepted me right away."

Barry did appreciate the support of the players and fans. He bought fifty bleacher seats for each of forty-two home games during the months of June, July, and August. The area was nicknamed the Bonds Squad. The tickets were donated to the Make a Family campaign for Adopt a Special Kid (AASK), which places needy children in caring homes.

In addition, Barry decided to donate $10,000 each year between 1993 and 1998 to AASK and $100 for each of his home runs, RBI, and stolen bases in each season. In 1993, Barry cohosted a Thanksgiving special on Prime Network to raise money for victims of the terrible fires in southern California. He signed baseballs and bats that were donated to the United Way to further help the fire victims. Barry never forgot the people who helped him when he was young. This was his way of saying thanks to the San Francisco community in which he grew up.

Barry Bonds now was known not only as a feared player with a bat in his hand but also as a charitable one. Movie producers began flocking to him with television and movie offers. Barry is a member of the Screen Actors Guild. He acted in the 1994 summer movie, directed by actor Daniel Stern, called *Rookie of the Year*. In addition, he was cast in the CBS-TV movie *Jane's House*. Barry has also been a guest on the Arsenio Hall, David Letterman, and Jay Leno shows. He has appeared on Fox TV's *In Living Color* and *Beverly Hills 90210*.

"I'm not into the glitzy stuff," Barry said. "I don't care about being seen places. I don't do the golf tournaments or hobnob with the stars. I do Arsenio or Jay Leno once in a while because they are friends of mine, they're in L.A., and I

Barry signs autographs for his fans.

can drive home afterwards. I don't care about commercials. My agent calls me and asks if I'd be interested in doing this or that, but I normally cut him off."

Despite Barry Bonds's reluctance to be part of the Hollywood lifestyle, the producers still continue to call. Stardom has not gone to his head. He realizes that baseball is a different game than show business: "Barbra Streisand just did that thing in Las Vegas. Do you know how big that was? I've never seen more celebrities! Well, if Barry Bonds says he wants to do a live performance, it's not as interesting. Because you see him 162 times [a season]. . . . [T]hey're [fans] getting a live performance from me every day."

In Barry's first season with San Francisco, the Giants jumped out to a big lead over the Atlanta Braves. However, due to injuries and some batting and pitching slumps on the Giants' roster, the Braves finally caught up. Barry did his best to help the Giants win the West Division.

Despite his efforts, the Giants weren't good enough. Atlanta won one more game than the Giants won. The Braves captured the West crown and headed to the World Series for the second straight year. Barry batted .336 with 46 homers and 123 RBI. All of these categories were career highs for him. In most seasons, he would have won the Triple Crown. "Nobody in the National League has had a year as good as Bonds in 1993 since Hack Wilson drove in 190 runs with a juiced up Depression ball in 1930," said baseball expert, author, and sportswriter Thomas Boswell. "Nobody in the National League has had back-to-back seasons like Bonds in 1992 and 1993 since Rogers Hornsby in 1928 and 1929."

For the third time in four years, Barry Bonds was named National League MVP. "I appreciate your help, because perception is very important," he told a sportswriter after

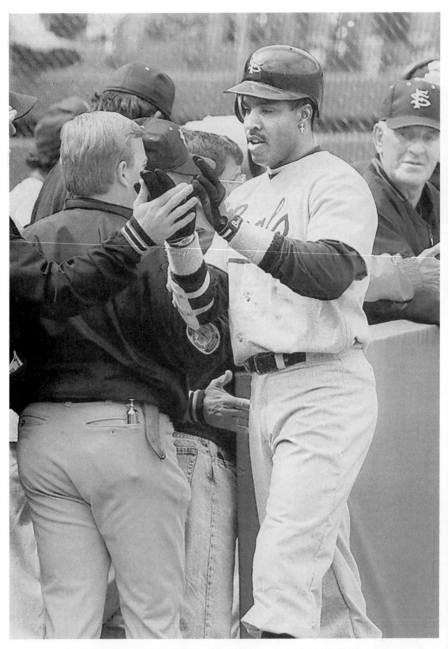

Teammates congratulate Barry after a home run against the Oakland As.

receiving the award. "I guess there are things I can't do by myself."

The 1993 season taught Barry that he could not win a divisional title by himself, despite statistics that even old-time ballplayers would admire. He quickly left the National League awards banquet, heading home to work out. The next season was just around the corner.

Chapter 5

The crowd of 17,458 at the Houston Astrodome were on the edge of their seats. Barry Bonds was coming up to bat. He was coming off his third Most Valuable Player honor, and he had made a pledge before the 1994 season to go for his fourth.

"So now I wonder: Can I win the fourth one?" said Barry before the season. "Is it possible?" He certainly was going to try, but he had other business to take care of in Houston as well. The Giants were struggling in the early part of the 1994 season. His teammates needed a lift. In this game, the Giants trailed, 1–0, in the fourth inning. Giants third baseman Matt Williams reached first base on a single with nobody out.

Astros' starting pitcher Pete Harnisch was on the mound. Harnisch was recovering from a nagging shoulder injury. He knew that he was facing the most dangerous hitter in the National League. He could not afford to get the ball close to the plate. The first pitch was wide of the plate. "Ball one!" yelled home plate umpire Bill Vanover. Harnisch was nervous at the thought of facing the explosive Bonds. He wiped the

Barry flinches after being hit on the elbow by a wild pitch.

sweat from his forehead. He put his foot back on the rubber part of the mound. A pitcher must always touch that piece of rubber before he makes a pitch.

Harnisch looked at his catcher for another sign. A catcher must let a pitcher know what type of pitch he would like so he isn't fooled by the toss. Harnisch got his sign. He wound up for the pitch. "Ball two!" yelled the umpire as the Astros' fans groaned. Was Harnisch going to throw a strike to Bonds?

On his next pitch Harnisch took a chance. It was close to home plate. Barry's eyes opened wide; he looked like a tiger ready to pounce on a deer. *Craaack!* His quick, short stroke snapped the baseball toward the left field wall only about fifteen feet off the ground. "Ohhhh," the Astros' crowd roared. The ball headed toward the bleachers in left field. Astros left fielder Luis Gonzalez raced back toward the wall. Too late! Barry's drive was so fast that it beat Gonzalez back to the bleachers. Some lucky Astros' fan now had a souvenir baseball from Barry Bonds! His two-run homer gave the Giants a 2–1 lead.

Harnisch was shaken up. It seemed he had lost some of his confidence. The next Giant at the plate was Willie McGee. He also hit one out to give San Francisco a 3–1 advantage. The Giants were rolling because of that one swing by Barry Bonds.

The Astros responded quickly to the Giants' power display. First, Jeff Bagwell stroked a double to the right field corner. Then Ken Caminiti smashed a double down the left field line off of San Francisco starting pitcher Bill Swift. The Giants' lead was cut to 3–2.

San Francisco needed to win this game to keep pace with the Los Angeles Dodgers, leaders of the Western Division by just half a game over the Giants. It was only May, but early games are just as important as games in September and

Although Barry is a celebrity, appearing in movies and television shows, he avoids reporters while he is at work on the baseball diamond.

October. Barry Bonds knew that. That's why he played 159 out of 162 games in 1993.

The Giants added a run in the fifth inning when Swift singled. He advanced to second base on a ground out. Matt Williams drove him home with a single. Now the Giants led 4–2, but the lead was not safe against the Astros.

Barry stepped up to the plate again in the top of the eighth inning. The crowd showed a sort of respect to him by booing as he got ready to hit.

Craaack! was the sound that echoed through the indoor stadium. The ball landed in the right center field bleachers; Barry had made another fan happy with a souvenir baseball. The Giants now had a comfortable three-run lead. Thanks to Barry's awesome power display, the Astros' fans were silent.

In the ninth, Giants pitcher Rod Beck came in to finish the game. He got the last three outs for the save; the Giants had kept pace with the first-place Dodgers. San Francisco had Barry Bonds to thank for that. His 2 homers and 3 RBI were the only runs the Giants really needed. It was truly a most valuable performance.

"This MVP [1993] is history," Barry said. "It doesn't mean a thing in 1994. I've got to work harder tomorrow. This was the first year that it started to get tough. I'm twenty-nine now, and each year I realize I have to work harder and harder. I played 159 games last season. In past years in Pittsburgh, [manager Jim] Leyland would pick spots to get me out of there against teams in the other division or against certain lefties.

"Last year, for the first time, I went longer and I could feel it in my legs. I felt my body tiring in September. So this winter, I'll work even harder than I ever have before."

Barry darts to first base. To stay in shape, he works out for five hours every day.

That was the real Barry Bonds, one of baseball's hardest workers. He was not going to be content with hitting 2 homers in one game; he had more work to do. Barry wanted to help the Giants get to the World Series. He so desperately wanted to win a World Championship.

"That's what you play this game for—to be the best," Barry said. "Late last season someone asked me if I could take it if the Giants lost. I told him I could take losing because I've experienced it at every level, from Little League to high school to Arizona State to Pittsburgh to San Francisco. All the teams I've played on, we made it right to the end and lost. So I know I can take losing. It's winning that I'm concerned about. My goal is that World Series ring. To get to that special level like my godfather [Willie Mays] or Mickey Mantle or Reggie Jackson, you have to win it all."

Barry Bonds is completely dedicated to the game of baseball. Some people, especially the media, have misunderstood him. Barry would rather be working out, playing ball, or taking batting practice than talk to someone about it. "My workout program right now is five hours a day," he said. "I've been asked by other players what I do to keep in shape. They can find out when I retire. Right now, it's between me and my trainer. My father can't believe what I go through. But when I see players who let themselves go, I can't stand it. When I went up to Vancouver last winter to shoot scenes for a movie, it was part of the deal with the film company that I would have five hours a day to work out. I'm not making forty-three million dollars to act."

There has been no other baseball player like him over the past five years, and Barry wants to keep it that way. "I really want that fourth [MVP] one," he says. "I want to do things no one else ever did. You ask me about my place in baseball history. I know that place. My godfather reminds me of it all the time."

It was a year of challenge for Barry, but he was going to work even harder to try for that fourth MVP in 1994. Barry Bonds has always been the first one to admit that his godfather has had an important place in baseball history. Willie Mays' all-around skills were among the best in the game. Many fans and sportswriters today believe that Mays' ability to run down a fly ball—when it seemed not humanly possible—was one of the most beautiful sights to see at a ballpark.

Bonds would also like to make his mark in baseball history. It is why he works out so hard every day, why he tries to be so perfect with each swing he takes, and why he has so much desire to work even harder for the fourth MVP. Barry missed out in 1994. But while many players were out of shape due to the strike that year and a late start for the 1995 season, Barry was working even harder during the off-season. His goal: to achieve his fourth MVP, a feat that many fans and sportswriters had thought impossible.

Chapter 6

Barry Bonds is important to the San Francisco Giants even when he is not hitting. Very few players have displayed such awesome skills both at bat and in the field. Many sportswriters and players believe that he may be one of the best outfielders ever to play the game. Like Michael Jordan, he is one of those rare individuals in sports. He always excites the fans, whether he is coming up to bat or throwing to home plate to try to catch a runner trying to score.

Barry brought this excitement to a game on August 2, 1994. Years from now, people who were witness to this event still will be talking about it. A crowd of 23,727 was on hand in San Francisco to root for the Giants against the Cincinnati Reds. The Giants were still trying to catch the Los Angeles Dodgers in the Western Division of the National League. Los Angeles led the Giants by a game and a half.

Barry Bonds knew that this game was important. He had been in a slump, but he was hitting the ball well again. The Giants needed his bat to be hot if they were to catch the Dodgers. The Reds moved ahead in the first inning when

Many believe that Barry Bonds is one of the best outfielders in the history of baseball.

Deion Sanders took first base after being hit by a pitch. Barry Larkin, the Reds' next batter, hit a home run to left center. The Reds led, 2–0.

Cincinnati made it 3–0 in the top of the third. Larkin doubled down the left field line and advanced to third on an error. Larkin scored when Reds shortstop Tony Fernandez grounded out into a force play at third base.

In the bottom of the inning, the Giants were at bat. Darren Lewis flied out to left field, but teammate Steve Scarsone walked. Barry Bonds was up next. The Giants crowd started to stir. Could he get the Giants back in the ball game?

Pete Schourek was on the mound for the Reds. He tried to throw a fastball outside to Barry Bonds. *Craaack!* It was a towering fly ball to right center. Reds right fielder Reggie Sanders raced toward the outfield wall. Sanders ran out of room. Barry's blast cleared the outfield fence by thirty feet. The Giants now trailed, 3–2.

The Reds were not going to make it easy for Barry and the Giants. In the fourth inning, Deion Sanders was able to hit a line drive over shortstop and into left center for an RBI single. Sanders's hit gave the Reds a 4–2 advantage.

The Giants scored a run in the fourth, too. Todd Benzinger singled to center field, but he was forced out at second base. Kirt Manwaring stroked a single to right field to put runners on first and third. Lewis hit a slow bouncer to shortstop and was able to beat the throw as a run scored.

San Francisco was still trailing 4–3 in the fifth when Barry came up to lead off the inning. Opposing pitchers were delighted that there were no Giants on base when Barry came up to bat. Schourek looked in at his catcher. *Craaack!* Bonds lifted a line drive toward Reggie Sanders in the right field again. Sanders hesitated at first, not sure if the ball would sink. It didn't. The ball flew over Sanders's head and into the

Barry hits a line drive to right field.

right field stands for Barry's second homer of the game. Now the game was tied 4–4. The Giants fans gave Barry Bonds a standing ovation. The Reds players were also impressed. "Barry Bonds is the best I've ever seen," Reds pitcher Jose Rijo said. "He can be pitched to but only very carefully. He's the best player overall."

Cincinnati pulled ahead of San Francisco in the seventh inning. Deion Sanders led off with a walk and moved to second base when Larkin sacrificed. Hal Morris was intentionally walked, and the bases became loaded when the Giants' third baseman misplayed a ground ball. The Giants were able to get one out with a run scoring, but Fernandez hit a line drive to left center. The hit scored two Reds runners. Cincinnati scored two more runs, for an 8–4 lead.

The Giants scored two runs in the bottom of the seventh inning. Lewis walked, and he advanced to third base on Scarsone's single to left field. Lewis scored; Scarsone moved to second base on a wild pitch. Then Barry Bonds stepped up to the plate. Reds pitcher Hector Carrasco threw another wild pitch. Scarsone scored from second base. It appeared that Barry had made the Reds pitcher nervous.

Barry Bonds could see that. Now the Giants trailed by just two runs. Carrasco knew that Barry had already hit 2 homers. He was going to try to keep the ball outside to Barry. He did, just enough. Barry whacked his curveball far, but not far enough. It was caught by the Reds' left fielder about fifteen feet from the wall.

Cincinnati continued to beat up on San Francisco's pitching. The Reds scored their ninth run of the day on Larkin's long home run to left field. The Giants had one last chance in the ninth, but the first two Giants made outs. San Francisco trailed by three runs. Barry Bonds was up at bat again.

Although he is the number one hitter in the National League, Barry will keep striving to improve until his team wins the World Series.

There were no Giants on base for Barry, but he surely was going to try to keep the game going.

Carrasco looked for a sign from the catcher. He was still going to keep the ball outside to Barry. Carrasco did, but this time it didn't work. It wasn't outside enough. *Craaack!* Bonds smacked a long high fly ball to left center. Deion Sanders, who is known to be one of the fastest players in baseball, started sprinting toward the wall. The Giants crowd roared. The ball disappeared over Sanders's head. It went into the stands in left center, for Barry's third homer of the day. It was the first time that he ever accomplished this feat.

"Barry Bonds, to me, is possessed," said Eric Anthony of the Seattle Mariners. "It's like he rolls out of bed, looks at himself in the mirror and knows he's the best. You can see it in his eyes. He has the total respect of everyone in the game. He's worth every penny he gets."

The Giants fans gave Barry Bonds another standing ovation. They cheered not only for his incredible feat, but also for his never-quit attitude. Barry is one of baseball's fiercest competitors.

Thanks to his third homer of the day, it appeared that the Giants had regained some spark. Williams hit a line drive into right field for a single, and the San Francisco fans roared louder. Darryl Strawberry hit a sharp ground ball toward second base. It seemed that it might slip into right field for another base hit, but it was smothered at second base. Strawberry was thrown out at first base. The Giants lost, 9–7.

Despite the loss, the 23,727 fans left Candlestick Park thrilled; it's not every day that a player hits 3 homers in a game! This is the type of performance that people expect from Barry Bonds when they pay their way into the ballpark. That's why he was the highest paid player in 1994. At any moment his bat or his glove or arm can ignite excitement. Barry Bonds never cheats the fans.

The Braves' Brett Butler said it best: "Willie Mays, Hank Aaron, Mickey Mantle. Their legends grew when their careers ended. When the numbers come out and Barry is out of the game, then he'll be in that same legend stage. There is no doubt Barry Bonds is the best player in baseball."

Career Statistics

Year	Team	G	AB	R	H	2b	3b	HR	RBI	SB	AVG
1985	Pr Will*	71	254	49	76	16	4	13	37	15	.299
1986	Hawaii*	44	148	30	46	7	2	7	37	16	.311
	Pirates	113	413	72	92	26	3	16	48	36	.223
1987	Pirates	150	551	99	144	34	9	25	59	32	.261
1988	Pirates	144	538	97	152	30	5	24	58	17	.283
1989	Pirates	159	580	96	144	34	6	19	58	32	.248
1990	Pirates	151	519	104	156	32	3	33	114	52	.301
1991	Pirates	153	510	95	149	28	5	25	116	43	.292
1992	Pirates	140	473	109	147	36	5	34	103	39	.311
1993	Giants	159	539	129	181	38	4	46	123	29	.336
1994	Giants	112	391	89	122	18	1	37	81	29	.312
Totals		1,281	4,514	890	1,287	276	41	259	760	309	.285

*Minor Leagues (statistics not included in totals)

Where to Write Barry Bonds

Mr. Barry Bonds
c/o San Francisco Giants
Candlestick Park
San Francisco, CA 94124

Index

Morris, Hal, 57

N

New York Mets, 29, 33, 36
New York Yankees, 15

O

Offerman, Jose, 9
Oliver, Al, 29

P

Parker, Dave, 29
Philadelphia Phillies, 29
Pittsburgh Pirates, 23, 27, 28, 29,
        31, 33, 35, 36

R

Rawley, Shane, 29
Rawlings Gold Glove Award, 15
Rijo, Jose, 57

S

St. Louis Cardinals, 31
San Francisco Giants, 7-9, 11-13,
        15, 19, 37, 41, 45, 47, 49,
        51, 53, 55, 57, 59

Sanders, Deion, 55, 57, 59
Sanders, Reggie, 55
Scarsone, Steve, 55, 57
Schourek, Pete, 55
Serra High School, 17
Stargell, Willie, 36
Strawberry, Darryl, 59
Swift, Bill, 47, 49

T

Torborg, Jeff, 36

V

Vanover, Bill, 45

W

Williams, Matt, 9, 11, 12, 45,
        49, 59
Wilson, Hack, 41
Wilson, Steve, 12